About the author

Zyrieda Denning was born and brought up in Brighton, then studied medicine in London. She trained as a surgeon, becoming a fellow of the Royal College of Surgeons in 1990. Her son was born in 1991. Five years later she became a Consultant at the Royal Hampshire County Hospital, and later started her own healthcare business.

Zyrieda had a daughter in 2008, who was originally not interested in healthy eating – this led Zyrieda to try a variety of methods: making up fairy tales to make healthy food more appealing, as well as starting a vegetable garden and going on trips to the local 'pick-your-own'. This worked so well, as her daughter started to eat much more healthily, that Zyrieda wanted to share her story with other parents to encourage their children to enjoy healthy food.

Max Denning, Zyrieda's son, wrote the Health Notes section in this book. He is studying medicine at the University of Oxford and has a diploma in sports nutrition.

In loving memory of Haldane Broby, 1966-2010

First published in Great Britain in 2012 by
The Book Guild Ltd
Pavilion View
19 New Road
Brighton, BN1 1UF

Designed and typeset by Marcus Duck

Printed and bound in Spain under the supervision of
MRM Graphics Ltd, Winslow, Bucks

A catalogue record for this book is available from
The British Library.

ISBN 978 1 84624 765 1

Alicia's
5-A-DAY
Magic Garden
with ABC Cookbook

Zyrieda Denning

Illustrated by Sarah Skeate

Book Guild Publishing
Sussex, England

Chapter 1

Alicia lived with her mum and dad in a small house in the country.

Every day, Alicia and her mum went out into the garden to plant or pick fruit and vegetables, and cooked tasty meals together with the food they had grown. But recently, her mum had become very busy teaching piano and singing at home, now that Alicia was old enough to play on her own.

It was a lovely warm day so Alicia went out by herself to collect fruit and vegetables from the garden.

She felt very lonely and longed for a friend.

Alicia took her basket and went to the apple tree, but as she picked the first apple, everything around her changed.

Her little house turned into a beautiful palace and there was a king and queen sitting on the balcony, drinking tea.

The gardens stretched as far as the eye could see.

The apple trees had been grown in the shape of an 'A', and around them were artichokes, asparagus, aubergines, apricots and avocado trees.

Then a boy approached her, walking with someone who appeared to be a chef, with a big 'A' on his apron and a little 'a' on his tall white hat.

'Hello!' said the young man to Alicia. 'Who are you?'

'My name is Alicia – and yours?'

'I am Albert and this is my chef, Adam,' he replied.

'Your chef?'

'Oh yes! My father, the King, has twenty-six chefs to look after the food that grows in our twenty-six gardens.

One garden and one chef for each letter,' explained Albert.

'Wow!' she exclaimed. Alicia was surprised to learn he was a prince – and even more surprised that they had twenty-six different chefs!

'You would like my gardens,' he said.

'I am sure they're beautiful,' smiled Alicia. 'Can I see them and pick some fruit?'

'Of course. I love picking fruit too! Do you enjoy cooking?'

'I love it!' said Alicia, very excited at meeting a new friend who enjoyed the same things as she did.

'Then let's collect some apples and take them to my kitchen and we can make an apple crumble together. But don't let my father see you – you shouldn't really be here!'

Alicia grabbed her basket, excitedly filled it with apples and ran with Albert into the kitchen, which was amazing. Everything was the same height as Albert and her.

Adam peeled and sliced all the apples. They arranged the slices and sprinkled cinnamon and nutmeg on top, then crumble mix, and Adam the chef placed the apple crumble in the oven.

Whilst it was cooking, Albert and Alicia made up a dance to pass the time. They danced and danced until the crumble was ready.

Meanwhile, Adam made them a healthy avocado and artichoke salad with some lovely sweet apricots on top.

When they had finished dancing, they sat down at the little table and gobbled up the salad. Then they ate the crumble topped with a slosh of custard, all washed down with apple juice.

But as Alicia ate her last mouthful, she found herself back at the apple tree outside her own house.

She wasn't quite sure what had happened, but she had certainly had a wonderful day with the prince and felt very happy!

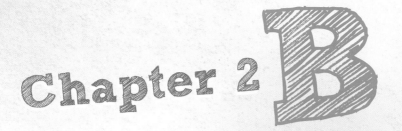

Chapter 2

The next day, Alicia went out again to pick some broccoli in the field near her house. She was thinking about the strange events of the day before and wished she could have another adventure. As she picked the broccoli, she found herself back in the beautiful magic palace gardens.

The broccoli plants in the palace garden were arranged in the shape of a letter 'B' and were surrounded by beans, blueberries, blackberries, banana trees, bay leaf plants and beetroot.

Alicia looked around and saw Albert with his father, the King. She quickly jumped behind the blackberry bushes and couldn't resist eating the plump, juicy berries as she hid.

She heard the King telling Albert that he had to meet a new friend called Catherine, the princess of the neighbouring city. The King hoped Albert would marry her when he was older, which made Alicia feel a bit sad.

When the King had gone, Alicia came out from behind the blackberry bush and ran over to Albert.

He took her into the 'B' kitchen to meet the chef, Ben, who was peeling bananas.

Alicia helped him chop the bananas, then added some milk, a little ice cream and put everything into a mixer. The result was a delicious banana milkshake.

Alicia and Albert drank the banana milkshake, whilst Ben the chef prepared the next dish – spaghetti Bolognese. To start off the delicious Bolognese sauce, chef Ben fried up some minced beef with onions and tomatoes. Albert and Alicia added mushrooms, a stock cube and a bay leaf for flavouring. Ben cooked all the ingredients until the sauce was just perfect.

They soon ate their scrumptious spaghetti and tasty sauce, followed by blackberry pie.

Alicia was so happy to be with Albert that she forgot about Catherine. As she finished the blackberry pie, once again she found herself back in the field near her own house, picking broccoli.

Chapter 3

The next day, Alicia went out to pick a cauliflower from her kitchen garden and just as she hoped, she found herself in Albert's magical 'C' garden.

There were cauliflowers, courgettes, carrots and cucumber plants; cranberries, cherries, coriander and even coconut trees.

The King was introducing Albert to Princess Catherine nearby, so Alicia hid amongst the cherry trees, listening carefully.

Albert asked Catherine if she liked his fruit and vegetable gardens.

Catherine said she did not care for them, and then he asked her if she enjoyed cooking.

Catherine was shocked at his question. 'Why, of course not! I never cook – we have chefs to do that!'

Albert went very quiet – he loved his gardens and he loved cooking and eating the delicious fresh food. Catherine didn't share his feelings.

Then Charlie, the 'C' chef, offered Albert and Catherine some cranberry juice, carrot sticks and cucumber slices as a snack.

There were some delicious dips to go with them, too. Catherine was not very impressed. She didn't like carrots and cucumbers.

Albert couldn't help imagining what she would grow up into if she didn't like vegetables – without carrots she wouldn't be able to see in the dark! He imagined her walking up the aisle of a packed great cathedral at a coronation ceremony. Then, just as she got to the steps leading up to the throne, she tripped and with her crown and sceptre flying, she fell 'splat' on her face.

'Next time, Princess,' Albert thought, 'you had better eat carrots and see where you are treading!'

Albert gave up on Catherine and said goodbye to her as he ran over to the 'C' garden in the hope that Alicia might be there.

She came out from behind the cherry trees, and together, they had fun collecting all the various fruits and vegetables around them. They then went cycling around the palace gardens to build up an appetite.

Afterwards, they went to join Charlie in the 'C' kitchen, and set about preparing a good healthy lunch.

Charlie prepared roast chicken and roast potatoes with coriander and boiled the cauliflower, courgettes, carrots and swede.

The children mixed together a cheese sauce for the cauliflower. Charlie put it all in the oven.

They mashed together the boiled carrots and swede, then added some pepper.

The children mixed eggs, flour, sugar and sunflower oil with grated carrots to make a delicious carrot cake with a letter 'C' on top for dessert.

As Alicia swallowed her last mouthful of carrot cake, she found herself transported back to her own garden, picking cauliflowers.

D Chapter 4

The next morning, Alicia went into the garden and looked around for something beginning with 'D', hoping that she would be transported back to the palace garden where she would find Albert. She saw some dill, and sure enough as she picked it, Alicia found herself in the magical garden surrounded by dates, dandelions and, of course, lots of feathery green dill.

Alicia hid behind the date palms and saw Albert walking along with his father, King Harold. The King was not happy that Albert had not only been rather rude to Princess Catherine, but also never wanted to see her again.

The King said that he needed to talk to Queen Eleanor about this, but in the meantime he suggested that Albert meet another princess called Eliza.

Albert thought it wise to agree and as soon as his father had gone he ran off to the date palms, hoping to find Alicia, who came out from behind the trees.

They were joined by Danny, the 'D' chef, and having collected their fruits, they all went into his kitchen.

Danny taught Alicia and Albert how to make easy dips, then some tasty pork and cabbage dumplings, followed by a date cake.

Albert and Alicia ate so many dumplings they nearly exploded. When they couldn't eat any more, they fell asleep and Alicia woke up in her own family garden.

Chapter 5

The next day Alicia needed to find something that began with 'E'. It wasn't that easy, but she remembered that an aubergine is also known as an egg plant - and plucked a large purple vegetable from the stem.

There were also elderberry bushes, endive plants and even a chicken pen for the hens to lay their eggs in. She hid behind the elderberry bushes and watched Albert meet Princess Eliza.

Eddie, the 'E' chef, came out from the kitchen to greet Albert and Princess Eliza. He offered them some chilled drinks and asked what Albert and Eliza would like to eat. Eliza wanted some crisps, chocolate and salted peanuts. 'Oh dear,' thought Albert, 'not a very healthy mixture!'

The children followed Eddie into the 'E' kitchen, where he made them an egg omelette with cheese and tomato. Albert mixed the eggs for the omelette, and to his horror, Eliza poured tons of salt into the omelette mix. She ate buckets of salt with everything! Albert thought that wouldn't be good for her, so prepared another omelette for Eddie to cook before Eliza had a chance to add any more salt.

Albert started to imagine what it would be like if she were to become queen.

He imagined her walking up to the coronation chair. Her heart had grown much weaker over the years and she could hardly make it up the steps. She looked so much older and was very wrinkly. She fell into the chair quite breathless and exhausted when she reached the top of the stairs.

No, Eliza was not for Albert, so Albert said goodbye as fast as he could and ran off to find Alicia. Together they went back to the kitchen, where Eddie took off his hat, waved his magic whisk and, from out of the hat, pulled a chicken and an egg.

Eddie cooked some egg plant with melted cheese on top in the oven. Alicia helped by making a big 'E' out of tomatoes to put on top of the cheese.

Whilst the egg plant was cooking, they talked and joked and drew pictures of chickens and eggs!

Then Alicia and Albert made an elderberry sorbet for dessert, carefully selecting their favourite fruits and mixing them together. As Alicia swallowed the last mouthful of her sorbet, once again she found herself transported back to her own garden.

F
Chapter 6

On the sixth day of the month, Alicia knew exactly what to look for and went out to pick some figs. As she had hoped, she found herself in the palace 'F' garden, surrounded by lush green fig trees and feathery fennel plants. There was a river running through the middle where fish were swimming in the clear water.

Alicia was picking and eating some of the figs when she saw Albert walking along with his mother, Queen Eleanor. She wanted him to meet yet another princess, this one was called Fiona.

Albert did not really want to meet any more princesses, as he was happy playing with Alicia, but had not dared to tell his parents about her yet. The Queen insisted that Albert meet Fiona and he reluctantly agreed. When they had finished talking, Fred, the 'F' chef, invited Albert to do some fishing in the river in the 'F' garden. Fred went and found two fishing rods and a net. Just then, out from behind the fig trees jumped Alicia.

'Can I come fishing too?' she asked.

Albert was delighted to see her again. They ran down to the riverbank, laughing and joking together. Fred took them and the fishing gear out in a rowing boat. Albert caught a salmon, and Alicia caught a trout. They rowed back to the kitchen with Fred.

Fred helped them to prepare the fish. He peeled and boiled some potatoes. The children placed the fish in a dish with some leeks, hard-boiled eggs and a lovely sauce. They mashed the potatoes with some butter and milk and spread the mash over the fish, topping it off with some grated cheese.

They sprinkled chopped parsley into an 'F' shape on top of their fish pie and placed it in the oven to cook.

While it was cooking, they turned their attention to dessert and made a delicious fig tart.

Alicia knew what was going to happen as soon as she finished her fabulous meal, so she said goodbye to Albert while she ate her helping of fig tart, before being whisked back home.

G Chapter 7

Luckily Alicia had a vineyard near her garden, so the next day she headed there to pick some lovely juicy grapes. As she picked a bunch from its vine, the vineyard transformed into the 'G' garden at the palace.

There were green beans, gooseberries, grapes and guava – not to mention garlic – everywhere.

Albert was walking with Fiona, so Alicia hid behind the gooseberry bushes and listened.

'Do you like my fruit and vegetable garden?' he asked.

'Oh yes, I like the gardens!' replied Fiona. 'But I do not like fruit and vegetables.'

Albert looked at her with surprise.

'What do you like to eat, then?' he asked.

'I love chocolate

cake, cream doughnuts, burgers and chips!' she answered, smiling at the thought of her favourite foods.

As Albert looked at Fiona his mind started drifting. He imagined a table piled high with all that stodgy food, with no fresh fruit or vegetables to enjoy with it. He imagined Fiona's tummy blowing up like a big balloon until she looked as if she would burst. He laughed out loud at this image in his head and decided that she was definitely not for him.

The thought of all those unhealthy, fattening foods made Albert feel a bit ill and so he rushed off towards the 'G' kitchen for something more healthy. Having seen Fiona leave, Alicia came out from behind the gooseberry bushes and caught up with Albert, who asked her if she would like to join him.

Gordon, the 'G' chef, was preparing dinner. While he made some garlic bread and a green bean salad, the children made tarts with grapes in the shape of a 'G' for decoration.

After dinner, as she polished off the last of the grapes, Alicia arrived back in her home garden.

She was pleased that Albert had not taken to Fiona.

Chapter 8

'Hmmm,' thought Alicia, 'the next letter is "H", what have we got here then?' Looking around the vegetable garden, Alicia found some horseradish and honeydew melons. When she stooped to pick up some fallen horse chestnuts, she found herself in the palace's 'H' garden.

Albert's father was asking why Fiona had run away.

'She didn't like fruit and vegetables, she only wanted to eat unhealthy food and I don't think it will do her any good!'

The King was not happy and suggested that instead he meet Princess Irene the next day. Albert was beginning to despair at having to see all these princesses when Harry, the 'H' chef, arrived to cheer him up. He wanted to collect some honey from the palace bees to put in some muffins he was going to bake.

Seeing Albert was downhearted, he said, 'What's the matter, young Albert?'

'The only girl I like is not a princess,' answered Albert.

'Oh dear!' said Harry. 'Who is she?'

'Her name is Alicia', replied Albert. 'But unfortunately she keeps disappearing each day.'

Alicia peered round from the horse chestnut tree, and Albert caught her eye. He was so happy to see her, he ran up and kissed her on the cheek.

'Why do you disappear whenever you finish your food?' he asked her.

'I'm not sure', replied Alicia. 'It's all magic and I really don't know how it works… Sometimes when I arrive I have to hide and listen because you don't want your parents to know about me!'

They went to the 'H' kitchen where Alicia and Albert helped Harry make the muffins. Harry put them in the oven and Albert and Alicia went outside to play with a bat and ball while they cooked.

They had a great time and then came back in to sit at their little table and eat the lovely warm, sweet muffins. They said their goodbyes while they were eating, knowing that Alicia would be disappearing once again when the meal was finished.

As soon as the last mouthful went down, Alicia found herself back in her garden with the horseradish plants.

Chapter 9 I

Alicia woke early the next morning and couldn't wait until she could go out into her garden again.

As soon as she could, Alicia ran out to look for something beginning with 'I' to continue her adventures in the alphabetical gardens of the royal palace. Her eyes fell upon an iceberg lettuce and as she picked it, she found herself back at the palace.

Then, to her dismay, she saw Prince Albert meeting Princess Irene.

Albert politely invited Irene to play. But Irene said she preferred to stay indoors and watch TV.

Albert imagined her as queen, with square eyes, a square body with a really funny square crown on an equally funny square head. Not for me, he thought!

Then Ivan, the 'I' chef, arrived and Albert went with him to the 'I' garden, leaving Irene glued to the television.

The 'I' garden had all kinds of different vegetables and fruits; apples, oranges, blackberries and blueberries. Enough to make lots of fruity ice cream. Albert just hoped Alicia would be there.

As Albert had hoped, Alicia was waiting and jumped out from behind a lychee tree. Then they both picked fruit, laughing and playing as they did so. They raced back to the kitchen with all the goodies they had collected.

'I'm first!' cried Albert.

They mashed the fruit until it was soft and smooth, mixed it with sugar and cream, then put it in the freezer.

In the 'I' kitchen, Ivan was preparing crispy lamb wrapped in iceberg lettuce. With lunch on the way, the happy pair went outside to compete in different kinds of races.

Ivan came out to be the judge. First they had a hopping race, and Alicia won easily.

Then they had a skipping race, which Alicia also won.

After this, they had an egg and spoon race, but this time Albert won. They followed this with an apple and spoon race, which they finished in a dead heat. They fell over the finishing line, helpless with laughter.

With the races all done, they went back into the kitchen to eat their crispy lamb and ice cream. On the last spoonful of ice cream, Alicia disappeared back to her own garden.

Chapter 10

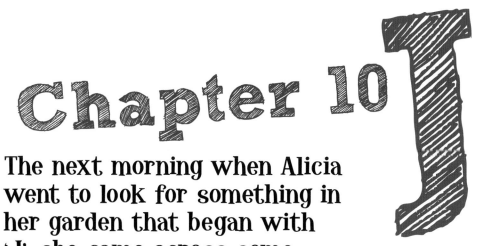

The next morning when Alicia went to look for something in her garden that began with 'J', she came across some beautifully scented jasmine flowers. 'Jasmine tea!' she thought. 'Just what I fancy.'

As she picked the white jasmine flowers, she was swept away to the palace 'J' garden.

Here, there were all kinds of fruit and flowers – jasmine, apples, pears, strawberries, raspberries, oranges, mangoes, lemons, bananas and pineapples, perfect for making juices.

This time, she couldn't see Albert. His parents were walking without him. They were discussing what to do about Albert's total lack of interest in all the princesses they had found for him.

'What shall we do next?' asked the Queen.

'Princess Karen is very beautiful,' suggested the King.

'Yes,' agreed Albert's mother. 'We will invite her tomorrow. He's bound to like Princess Karen!'

Then Alicia, who was hiding, heard a whisper behind her – it was Albert. He was also hiding and listening to his parents' conversation.

As his parents walked away, Albert realised that Alicia must have been watching and listening to him talking to all the different girls.

He asked Alicia what she had seen and heard.

'Oh dear!' he said. 'Why didn't you tell me you knew?'

'You never asked,' replied Alicia.

Albert was most embarrassed and told Alicia that all he wanted to do was to play with her. 'Maybe I should introduce you to my parents?' he said.

Alicia smiled and pointed out that she was not a princess and his parents would not approve. 'Let's wait,' she suggested. She didn't want to be banished from his magic gardens if they found out about her visits.

Alicia and Albert picked up all the fruit they could carry and took it to John, the 'J' chef, who cut a couple of the fruits in half for them to squeeze into juice, whilst he brewed up some jasmine tea.

John then liquidised all the remaining fruits and arranged them in glasses as if they were a liquid rainbow, starting with deep violet blackberry juice, then a paler purple bilberry juice, followed by blue blueberry juice, then green lime juice, then orange orange juice and red strawberry juice!

John then made them a really big mystery meal and they tied a scarf over their eyes to avoid seeing what it was, but neither of them was able to guess from the taste alone.

Finally, as Alicia tasted the very last jewel-coloured fruit juice, she was carried away on a rainbow back to her own garden.

K
Chapter 11

Alicia knew just what to pick on the eleventh day of the month, 'K' being the eleventh letter of the alphabet. She headed for a large kiwi tree and as she stretched out to grab the fruit, she was transported to the 'K' garden of the royal palace where all the kiwi trees were arranged in the shape of a letter 'K'. Alicia hid behind one of the trees.

She heard Albert being introduced to Karen and could see them at the palace door. Karen had beautiful wavy long blonde hair.

'Would you like to come for a walk around my fruit garden?' Albert asked.

'No thanks,' she replied. 'I am not into exercise. Do you have any computer games we can play? I love electronic toys!'

'My dad has a computer,' Albert replied. 'But it's a beautiful day. Wouldn't you prefer to be outside?'

'I'd much rather play on a computer!' replied Karen.

Karl, the 'K' chef, went out to greet Albert and Karen. He offered them a tray of fruit, nuts and bananas as well as a range of wholegrain sandwiches with delicious fillings.

'No thanks,' said Karen, turning her nose up at all the scrumptious goodies. 'I prefer to eat take-aways with my friends. Can't you cook up some burgers and fries so we can play on the computer?'

Albert imagined what it would be like if she were to become queen.

He imagined Karen in years to come. She would have round eyes on spring stalks with giant spectacles hanging on the end of her nose. Some of her beautiful hair would have fallen out and her crown would be perched on top of her nearly bald head.

Albert started laughing out loud at the horrible thought and hastened to try and say goodbye to the girl crazy about electronic games.

Alicia sighed at the sight of her friend laughing, not realising that it wasn't because he was enjoying himself. She picked some more kiwi fruits and Karl, the 'K' chef, invited her into the kitchen to make a kiwi tart. She rolled out the dough whilst Karl prepared vegetable kebabs for her.

Karl peeled and sliced the kiwi fruit and cooked the pastry base. Alicia poured a creamy filling flavoured with lime and vanilla over the base and arranged the kiwis in a 'K' shape. She used heart-shaped baking trays and made two tarts. Alicia ate one of the tarts and left the other one for Albert, who was still trying to get away from Karen. Then Alicia vanished back to her house.

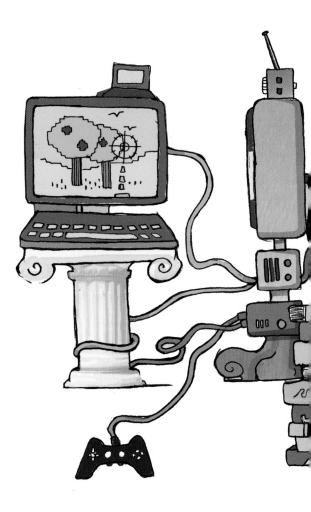

As soon as Albert could, he rushed out to the 'K' garden to find Alicia. Karl the chef showed him the heart-shaped kiwi tart Alicia had left for him. He felt very sad when he realised that she was gone and he would not see her that day.

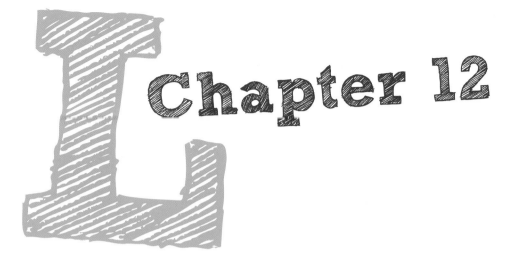

Chapter 12

The next day, Alicia went to pick a lemon and off she went to the palace 'L' garden, where lemon and lime trees were all arranged in 'L'-shaped orchards.

Albert ran towards her and gave her a big hug. 'I must tell my parents about you. I don't want to meet any more silly princesses.'

Alicia was delighted, for she loved seeing Albert each day. But she also liked going back home and being in her own house with her parents.

'Not yet', Alicia replied. 'Your parents might not accept me, and that would spoil our fun forever!'

Albert reluctantly agreed.

So they picked some more lemons and limes from the trees and took them to Leo, the 'L' chef.

Leo cooked them a delicious seafood linguine.

They drank lemonade made from fresh lemons and limes.

Leo was a very talented chef who also knew how to build things.

Albert asked him what he could make and Leo suggested a tree house.

So they went outside, found some wood and Leo helped them build a fabulous tree house.

When it was finished, they all climbed in and started to mix lemons and limes in a bowl with the eggs, sugar and cream and spread the thickened mixture over a biscuit base to make lemon and lime cheesecake. They decorated the edge with strawberries and wrote the letter 'L' on the top with lemon zest.

It was delicious. Albert was so happy to be playing in the tree house and cooking with Alicia that he forgot all about his parents' attempts to find him a princess.

After eating the cheesecake with Albert, Alicia found herself back at home, also feeling very happy with the world.

Chapter 13

Alicia went out to pick a marrow underneath a mandarin tree and found herself in the palace 'M' garden. She was surrounded by Chinese pagodas and ornate fountains as well as marrows, mandarins, mangoes, melons and mulberries, all arranged in lines making up the letter 'M'.

She heard Albert talking to his mother, Queen Eleanor, so Alicia hid behind the mandarin tree.

Eleanor wanted Albert to meet Princess Madeleine.

Albert started to tell her about a lovely girl called Alicia who was not a princess.

Queen Eleanor was outraged. 'You can't possibly be friends with an ordinary girl!' she shouted.

Albert gave up trying to explain how much he liked Alicia. He knew it wouldn't go down too well. So he wondered with horror how many more princesses he would have to meet. He reluctantly agreed to meet Princess Madeleine and his mother finally went back to the palace. With his mother gone, he hopped, skipped and jumped over to the 'M' garden, hoping Alicia would see him playing and come out of her hiding place.

He looked around the nearest mandarin tree and found her. 'Boo!' he said. This time, he surprised her.

They picked the mandarins from the trees and melons from where they lay on the ground.

Mike, the 'M' chef, came whistling along a path and they followed him to the 'M' kitchen, where he treated them to a smoothie made with fresh mangoes.

Alicia and Albert tried their hand at making different flavours of smoothies with strawberries, vanilla and cocoa.

Mike sliced a marrow from the garden in two and gave one half to Alicia and the other half to Albert.

They quickly set about scooping out the insides. The next step was to add some olive oil, crushed garlic and a light sprinkling of rock salt. Not forgetting the rosemary.

In the meantime, Mike got on with marinating some chicken breasts in olive oil and soy sauce.

The chef took the marrow halves prepared by Alicia and Albert and together with the marinated chicken, put everything into the oven for thirty minutes.

Whilst the chicken and marrows were cooking away, Mike made the youngsters a fruit medley with meringues, mandarins, mangoes, melons and strawberries. Albert and Alicia gulped down all the goodies and as the last mouthful vanished, so did Alicia.

N Chapter 14

The next day, Alicia went to pick a nectarine from its tree and found herself surrounded by all kinds of trees with nuts on them. Cashew nuts, walnuts, almonds, pistachio and nutmeg all flourished. The rows of nut trees were all lined up in the shape of the letter 'N'.

As arranged, Albert was introduced to Princess Madeleine at the palace. She wore a long dress with sleeves that covered part of her dainty long gloves and had a medieval veil over her head and face. Beneath the veil she had very pale skin.

Albert invited her out into the 'N' garden, but she refused.

'It's too sunny,' she said, 'and I don't want to ruin my skin. It will be all wrinkled when I get older.'

'A little bit of sun is good for you,' answered Albert, 'and it won't ruin your skin. On the contrary, it helps to make vitamin D. You only have to avoid strong sun and getting burnt.'

Then Nick, the 'N' chef, arrived to welcome Madeleine with a tray holding two almond and pistachio nut-flavoured milkshakes.

'Oh no!' exclaimed Madeleine. 'I can't drink milk.'

Albert was already shocked to hear that Madeleine didn't like to go outside in the sun and now it was even worse. She wouldn't drink milk either.

Albert suddenly had a vision of Madeleine walking along a corridor with wobbly arms and legs, as he knew that not going outside and not drinking milk was a very unhealthy lifestyle that wasn't good for strong, healthy bones.

Because Madeleine stayed indoors, Alicia had to spend her day in the 'N' garden on her own.

So she climbed up some trees with low-hanging branches and gathered up bunches of nuts which she took into the kitchen for Nick.

Nick felt a bit sorry for her, having to play on her own, so he asked her to help him bake a nut loaf to go with some new potatoes and some green vegetables. First, Alicia mixed up a selection of chopped nuts including Brazils, cashews and walnuts. Nick cooked onions in oil for five minutes and then he added mushrooms and garlic. He sprinkled on some flour and stirred until the mixture was sizzling, then stirred in Alicia's chopped nuts, lots of breadcrumbs and an egg. Together they shaped the mixture into a loaf and coated all the sides with flour. The loaf was then placed in a little oil on a baking tray and cooked until golden brown. They tucked in and afterwards, Alicia ended up back home, wishing she had seen Albert.

Chapter 15

The next day was beautifully warm and perfect for picking oranges, as 'O' was the next letter of the alphabet. Alicia climbed into the dark green leaves of the orange tree, surrounded by hundreds of juicy ripe oranges. She peered out from the leaves and saw she was in the palace 'O' garden.

From her unusual perch, sitting high up in the orange tree, she saw Albert walking towards the orange grove with his father, the King.

King Harold was worried that his son did not like any of the beautiful princesses he and Queen Eleanor had invited to the palace.

He thought that maybe all the princesses were not pretty enough for Albert, so he suggested that Albert should meet Princess Pearl, who was exceptionally beautiful. Not wanting to disappoint his father, Albert eventually agreed to meet her.

His father went back to the palace and Albert started to look everywhere amongst the orange trees for Alicia. But he couldn't see her anywhere. This was because Alicia was high above his head, in the middle of the leaves.

39

When Albert stood still for a moment beneath the orange tree that Alicia was hiding in, she carefully dropped off her branch, and fell right on top of him. 'Surprise!' she cried.

Albert was very surprised indeed!

'Where did you come from?' he gasped.

'I was hiding up there on a branch, hidden by leaves!' she explained.

Oscar, the 'O' chef, found them sprawled on the path beneath the orange tree before they had a chance to get up. 'What on earth are you two doing down there?' he laughed.

Albert rushed to the rescue. 'We were just looking for fallen oranges,' he explained, not wanting Oscar to think Alicia was the sort of girl to jump out of trees.

'Well, don't just lie there staring at them. Start filling those baskets with oranges and bring them into the kitchen!'

As soon as they did what he said, Oscar quenched their thirst with some fresh orange juice and then delivered up his special meal of the day. It was orange and carrot soup, followed by duck à l'orange with potato and spinach gratin, followed by an orange surprise sorbet and ice cream collection decorated with a terrific selection of fruits from the forest. He even made oatmeal and raisin cookies for an extra treat.

Having tried all the lovely desserts, Alicia returned home.

Chapter 16

The next day, Alicia went out to collect a pumpkin from her back garden. As she dragged her garden fork along the ground, she was back at the palace in the 'P' garden. There were potatoes, parsley, peas, parsnips, pears, pumpkins and peppers all around her. Each different type of fruit and vegetable was arranged in a 'P'-shaped plot.

She hid behind the giant pear tree in the middle of the garden and watched as 'her' prince was introduced to Princess Pearl.

Pedro, the 'P' chef, appeared on the scene and offered the prince and princess some pineapple juice.

'No thank you,' she replied, 'I don't like fruit. Do you have any fizzy drinks?'

Albert imagined what Pearl would look like as queen without her pearly-white teeth. She would look really funny with an empty gaping-wide mouth, a cake on her head instead of a crown and a set of false teeth in her right hand instead of a sceptre.

He could imagine all her teeth dissolving in a bucket of fizzy drink. All for the lack of some tasty fruit juice!

Oh no, there was no way he could marry her.

He started laughing as he imagined her false teeth running and rattling after him.

Pearl couldn't understand what was so funny.

They walked around the garden as she gulped down a fizzy drink. Then, without warning, she let out a big burp.

That was it, thought Albert. No way!

Whilst this pantomime was in progress, Alicia went about her business collecting the vegetables, herbs and fruit from the 'P' garden.

When her errand was done, Peter the 'P' chef helped her make a pie with the pumpkin that she had brought him in her basket. She mashed the pumpkin with cinnamon and nutmeg and helped make a 'P' shape out of the pastry as decoration. Then Peter carved a Halloween-style face out of another pumpkin and made it into a lantern with a lit candle inside it. Alicia, all on her own, sat down in the 'P' kitchen to a feast of pork with red, yellow and green peppers, roast parsnips with honey, peas and new potatoes. Then there were poached pears or pumpkin pie for dessert.

As soon as Albert was able to escape from Pearl, he ran over to the 'P' kitchen – but Alicia had gone.

So he returned to the 'P' garden play area with its swings and roundabouts and obstacle courses, but it was not the same without Alicia. He really missed her.

Chapter 17

The next day, Alicia's mother asked her to pick some quince pears to make jam. She rushed out into the garden as 'Q' was the next letter of the alphabet and she couldn't wait to see Albert again.

As she stretched out to pick her first quince fruit, she found herself in the palace 'Q' garden. There was a whole orchard of quince trees, but as was to be expected with a 'Q' garden, it was also very quirky. There was a quaint vegetable garden, which was very old-fashioned looking and divided into quarters. Neat little rows of vegetables such as carrots, beans, Brussels sprouts and onions grew in each section.

Hidden from view between two rows of runner beans, Alicia saw Albert talking to his mother, Queen Eleanor. They were discussing Princess Pearl. Albert was adamant that he did not want to see her again.

'There are only a few more princesses left in all the continent,' his mother explained. 'Surely, you must like someone!'

In despair, his mother persuaded Albert that the next day he must meet Rowena, a truly lovely princess from a neighbouring kingdom.

The Queen walked back to the palace, despairing at her son's lack of interest in princesses.

Now that he had been left to his own devices, Albert ran over to the 'Q' garden for some space of his own and to look for the girl whose company he really enjoyed – Alicia.

Albert looked all around the quince trees but couldn't

see Alicia anywhere. Then, as his gaze wandered over to the nearby vegetable patch, he spotted his friend. She was almost hidden from view amongst the runner beans.

There was someone else in the 'Q' garden. It was Quazimodo, the 'Q' chef. His nickname was 'Quasi' (meaning 'almost') because he sometimes took shortcuts with his cooking efforts when no one was looking. His quasi-cooking technique was to slip frozen foods into a microwave. A real chef would say that was cheating!

Quasi offered to help Albert and Alicia collect the quince pears. When they had a large batch of fruit, they took it back to the 'Q' kitchen. Quasi couldn't cheat on making quince marmalade because it doesn't come in a frozen packet from the

44

supermarket. He had to go through the proper process of boiling up the fruit with sugar.

Whilst the quince marmalade was bubbling away, Quasi decided to play it safe and go for a quiche using the other vegetables they had collected in the garden. He thought that would be a quick and easy way to rustle up something for his princely guest and Alicia. The inseparable friends then rolled out some pastry and mixed the eggs to help make the quiche.

Whilst the quiche was baking, they went outside to play badminton. After a terrific game and having worked up quite an appetite, they returned to eat the warm, savoury quiche and taste the sweet marmalade before Alicia returned home.

R Chapter 18

The next day, Alicia went out to dig up some radishes. With the first bright red radish popping out of the ground followed by its long white trailing root, she found herself in the royal 'R' garden.

There were radishes, rhubarb, raspberries and rosemary. There was also a lovely collection of different coloured rhododendrons. Each group of similarly-coloured red, white, pink or purple-coloured rhododendron bushes was laid out in the shape of an 'R'.

The King and Queen were standing side-by-side amongst the rhododendrons with the beautiful Princess Rowena. They introduced Rowena to Albert and left the two youngsters to get to know one another.

Albert invited Rowena to look at his 'R' garden and she obliged, smiling.

Robert, the 'R' chef, was sent out by the Queen to bring them a couple of glasses of raspberry juice.

Rowena drank her raspberry juice out of politeness but she preferred to suck away at a secret hoard of sweets she had hidden in her pockets. As each sweetie went down her throat, so another sweet paper floated down to earth. The radish patch was soon littered with them. Soon there were sweet wrappers all over the rosemary and rhubarb as well.

Albert couldn't believe his eyes. 'Don't you want to keep the rubbish for recycling?' he asked.

'No!' she replied. 'A servant will pick them up after me.'

Albert was shocked at her attitude. He imagined her walking up the aisle to the throne with a procession following on behind. Her crown was perched on top of her head and he was walking next to her. They were surrounded by piles of rubbish and as part of her procession, there were two mice, two rats and two foxes to help hold her train above the litter.

He couldn't help turning his nose up at the thought of how awful the smell would be.

Rowena was definitely not for him.

Albert quickly said goodbye to Rowena and ran over to where Alicia was collecting her fruits, vegetables and herbs in the 'R' garden.

Robert reappeared and offered them lunch in his kitchen.

They feasted on roast lamb with roast potatoes cooked in rosemary. There was cauliflower cheese, carrots, peas and roast parsnips, followed by a raspberry fool that Albert and Alicia had helped to prepare.

As soon as Alicia dipped into the creamy raspberry fool, she was transported back home and that was the end of their adventure for the day.

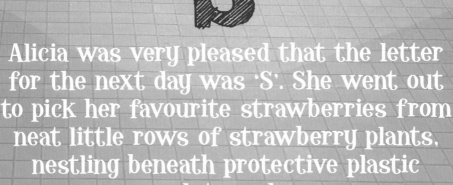

Chapter
19

S

Alicia was very pleased that the letter for the next day was 'S'. She went out to pick her favourite strawberries from neat little rows of strawberry plants, nestling beneath protective plastic polytunnels.

As she lifted the plastic covering from the pretty strawberry plants, she found herself in the 'S' garden of the palace.

The garden had a wide range of super 'S' plants including strawberries, spinach, squash, sweetcorn, sunflowers, sultanas and satsumas. The squash were yellow and orange whilst the sweetcorn was white and yellow.

The sunflowers were incredibly tall and they easily hid Alicia, so she was able to listen to Albert talking to his mother.

The Queen was extremely unhappy that Albert did not like any of the girls they had lined up for him, and there were only two possibilities left.

One of these was Princess Tiana and Albert had no choice but to agree to meet her the next day.

Thoroughly fed up, Albert went to the 'S' garden where Alicia was picking up a squash.

Sid the chef came out from his 'S' kitchen to suggest that he could cook a sizzling beef steak with creamed spinach, sweetcorn and a mash made from squash and potatoes.

Albert and Alicia couldn't resist the temptation and hurried along to the kitchen to tackle the steak.

In order to build up a serious appetite, they went for a dip in the palace swimming pool. The exercise made them really hungry, so they finished the swim and dried themselves before rushing back for their steak treat.

When Sid had cooked the vegetables, Alicia and Albert mashed the squash and potato together then added pepper, herbs and some soft, cooked onions.

Then at long last they sat down and ate their delicious meal, well worth all the preparation.

Sid then brought out a strawberry trifle, made with sponge cake, lots of strawberries, jelly and custard.

It was decorated with strawberry slices in a swirly 'S' shape.

As they finished the trifle, Alicia found herself back at home.

Alicia went out to pick tomatoes in her greenhouse. Outside it was a crisp and cool day for the time of year.

As Alicia grabbed hold of a really ripe red tomato, she found herself in the royal 'T' garden.

There was a wonderful selection of tomatoes in the greenhouses and turnips, thyme, turmeric and tarragon herbs in the ground outside.

As Alicia admired all the different herbs, she saw Princess Tiana arriving accompanied by a convoy of five large stretch limos. She was very pretty and elegantly dressed. 'Oh dear,' thought Alicia. 'This is competition!'

No sooner had she arrived than Tiana excused herself to go to the bathroom. As she went into the palace, she turned on all the lights even though it was daylight outside.

She stayed in the bathroom for what seemed like ages.

When she finally came out, she had obviously been putting on even more make-up.

Unfortunately, she had also left the hot water tap running and the bathroom lights on.

Albert had to follow in her footsteps turning off all the lights and the hot water tap. He was not impressed. Royal as

his parents were, they had taught him to conserve water and be fuel-efficient for the sake of the planet.

The King had even installed solar panels and rainwater recycling systems on the palace roof tops. Yet this young princess could not care less about wasting water and energy.

Albert again asked Tiana if she wanted to go outside to play.

'Oh, no!' she replied. 'I'm too cold – you really do need some heating in this palace.'

'Heating?' repeated Albert. He was quite warm. 'Would you like a cardigan or a coat, perhaps?'

'No, thank you. I like my own clothes just as they are!'

'Or lack of them!' thought Albert. He imagined what it would be like if she were to become a queen. There would be no fossil fuels left on the planet, and she would be spinning around with her arms and legs outstretched like a windmill to generate some more electricity!

He started laughing at the thought. Once again, the princess was not for him.

So he said goodbye and ran out to join Alicia in the 'T' garden.

They carried on collecting tomatoes, turnips and tarragon from the garden and took them to the 'T' kitchen for Tom, the 'T' chef.

He made tomato juice for them to drink.

Then, using the tomatoes as a starting point, Tom decided to cook a tomato, tuna and sweetcorn pizza for lunch. He brought out some pizza base mix, and then the children rolled it out and spread tomato puree on it. They then added tuna, sweetcorn, peppers and mozzarella cheese on top. It only took about ten minutes to cook.

Biting into the last slice of the pizza, Alicia found herself back in her own greenhouse, surrounded by her tomato plants.

Chapter 21

In the morning, Alicia went out to her garden as usual to see her really special tree that grew Ugli fruit, a cross between a grapefruit, an orange and a tangerine. Reaching for one of the fruits was enough to send her off to the palace 'U' garden.

There was only one Ugli tree in the palace garden. But of course the Ugli tree is very rare, even for a royal palace.

Then she spotted Albert – being lectured to by his parents, the King and Queen.

Albert insisted that he did not like Princess Tiana and the King and Queen were dismayed. 'There is only one princess left!' exclaimed the Queen. 'Princess Violet…'

Albert had to agree to meet her the next day, and then he stormed off to the 'U' garden in the hope of finding Alicia.

She was hiding amongst the undergrowth of the 'U' garden so as not to be seen by the King and Queen.

Then Uppity, the 'U' chef, came into the garden and gave them a lift up into the branches to get the fruit from the Ugli tree. He passed up a basket to where they were perched amongst the leaves and they filled it up in no time. Uppity took the fruit to the kitchen where he squeezed it to make a mixed fruit smoothie. He decided to make his signature dish, which no one had ever heard of. It was Ukrainian holubchi, which was minced meat and rice rolled in cabbage leaves, with bacon strips on top.

Uppity also prepared some peppers stuffed with mince and rice.

The children decided to make an upside-down cake and started to mix the ingredients, using Ugli and pineapple slices to make it unique.

The chef placed the upside-down cake in the oven to cook. When it had cooled down, Alicia and Albert decorated the top with a string of glacé cherries in the shape of a 'U'.

Then they sat down to eat.

It was all delicious, but as the last cherry slithered down her throat, so Alicia found herself back home.

Chapter 22

Alicia thought hard the next morning about what she could come up with for the letter 'V'. The alphabet was nearly finished, and she didn't know what would happen to her magic trips to the palace once she had run out of letters.

She looked all around the garden and finally she spotted some vanilla pods – perfect! As she collected the long thin pods, she found herself in the palace 'V' garden.

The garden had plants arranged in a 'V'-shape. Around the vanilla there were delicate flowerbeds with violets for food colouring and bright blue veronica. A drooping canopy of vines hung from the 'V' garden wall, providing a convenient place for Alicia to hide. As she stood pressed against the wall behind the vines, she hoped no one could see her. But Alicia could still peer out between the brown branches and green leaves.

From this vantage point, she could see Princess Violet arriving. Princess Violet had heard rumours that Albert preferred his garden to toys, and that indeed he did not have many toys. She had also heard that most of those he

had were made from forest-friendly wood and not brightly coloured plastic like hers!

So she brought along a second car loaded full of big, bright, plastic toys for them to play with, thinking that would please the impoverished prince.

When Albert asked the princess if she wanted to go out to play in the gardens, she replied, 'Oh, yes! That would be great. I've brought along a few toys for us to play with!'

'A few?' asked Albert looking at the carload of toys, surprised.

'Oh yes,' she said. 'I have mountains of toys in my palace.'

Albert started imagining how she would dispose of all these plastic toys when she grew up and no longer needed them. He pictured himself having to dig a great big hole to put all the unwanted toys in, but it filling up, growing and growing until it was as big as a volcano. Then, when it could grow no more, it erupted with streams of multi-coloured plastic toys flying into the air and molten plastic rolling down its slopes.

Violet seemed so spoilt. He could imagine her as queen, wearing a big bright-coloured plastic crown on her head. No, she was definitely not for him. So he left her with her toys and went instead to find Alicia in the 'V' garden.

Victor, the 'V' chef, came out from his kitchen to look for them. He was carrying two bowls of vegetable soup which Alicia and Albert ate along with some delicious crusty bread. 'Do come in for a vanilla yogurt drink when you've finished and you can help me make a vanilla cake.'

They cheered and went into the kitchen to help Victor make the vanilla cake with strawberry jam in the middle. Alicia and Albert couldn't resist, although they knew the end of the meal would mean the end of their day's adventures. Eventually, as Alicia ate the last mouthful of cake, she found herself back at home.

Chapter 23

The next day was sunny and very hot, so Alicia went out to collect some watercress from the stream at the side of her house. It was the perfect 'W' food for the day; refreshing, cool and full of vitamins.

As she had hoped, when she bent down to pick it up she found herself in the palace 'W' garden. There were walnut trees and watermelon plants, all arranged to make up the shape of a 'W'.

In the water meadows, there was watercress. Ideal with an egg sandwich on walnut bread. The prince was sitting under one of the walnut trees with both his parents, insisting that he really didn't like any of the princesses they had presented to him.

Instead, he was trying his hardest to persuade them to meet this friend Alicia whom he really, really liked.

His parents were not very pleased that Albert was disobeying them in favour of an ordinary girl, but they only wanted him to be happy so they agreed to meet her for lunch.

Albert skipped with joy and ran into the watermelon area of the 'W' garden, where he found Alicia. 'My parents would like to meet you tomorrow!' he cried . 'Then, if they like you, I can marry you, and we can live here in the palace together!' He was so excited, he didn't see Alicia's expression change.

She was definitely not ready to leave her mum and dad and go and live with someone else, no matter who he was and no matter how much she liked him.

Alicia agreed to meet the King and Queen, but told Albert she definitely could not marry him for several years to come at least!

Albert looked a bit sad. 'Well, just come and meet my parents tomorrow and see how that goes,' he said.

Rather more subdued than usual, they went into the 'W' kitchen and drank some crushed watermelon juice.

William, the 'W' chef, was making them some tortilla wraps filled with chicken, bacon, spinach and avocado. They had rice, watercress and walnut salad as a side dish.

Meanwhile, the children made a walnut and banana cake under William's watchful eye.

When it was all ready, they sat down to sample their cooking efforts.

It was delicious and as soon as it had all gone, Alicia found herself back home. She was always disappointed to leave Albert, but the idea of staying with him in the palace forever made her a little relieved to be at home with her parents again.

Chapter 24

The next day, Alicia was extremely nervous. She was worried about meeting the King and Queen.

She put on her prettiest dress and smartest shoes. With today being such a special day, she didn't want to spoil her outfit by doing any gardening. So she resisted collecting anything, but went over to the Xigua watermelons and ran her fingers over the shiny surface to see if that would do the trick – and it did!

Albert was there, waiting to greet her. He took her by the hand and led her indoors to meet his parents. Unfortunately, Alicia was so nervous she forgot to curtsey. Instead, she froze in an awkward silence.

Albert's parents started asking her a stream of questions that she couldn't answer. All she could think about was her own mum and dad, and how much she would rather be with them.

To break the ice, Albert suggested that they went into the royal banqueting hall for lunch.

As they sat down to eat, Alicia could see all the different chefs she had met from the 'A' to 'W' kitchens hurrying about. There were even some extra chefs she hadn't met before. It was all a bit bewildering!

Even when Xanthi the 'X' chef brought out a trolley selection of every type of melon one could imagine – including Alicia's favourite Xigua melon – she was so nervous that she couldn't decide which ones to eat.

Then they were served up a delicious seafood paella with mussels, salmon, prawns, squid and halibut on a bed

of saffron rice. To add a touch of flavouring there were some onions, red and green peppers plus a little sweetcorn with cloves and a caper or two added in for good measure.

Alicia looked at the marvellous food, but she was so uncomfortable in these splendid surroundings that she didn't know where to start. The food just sat there, staring back up at her.

The meal progressed at a very slow pace and Alicia hardly ate anything.

Eventually, the main course was removed from the table and replaced by a delicious concoction of strawberries, raspberries and redcurrants drizzled with melted white chocolate.

Despite her nerves, Alicia couldn't resist the bright berries dessert. As soon as her lips touched her spoon, she was swept back into her own garden.

For the first time she was actually happy to be back home, away from the palace.

Chapter 25

Alicia felt terrible that she had let Albert down so badly when she had been invited to the palace for lunch with the King and Queen. She wandered aimlessly about her own house, worrying about the situation. Eventually, she went out into her garden to clear her head and think about all the magical gardens she had seen at the palace. She realised what a jam she was in and wondered how she could sort it out.

Then her eyes settled on a yam. Maybe the yam was the way to resolve the jam! If she rubbed the yam, it would transport her to the 'Y' garden in the palace, she would find Albert and apologise for her behaviour.

As she touched the yam, as she had hoped, she found herself in the palace 'Y' garden.

She waited and watched and waited some more.

Then she spotted Albert protesting to his parents that in spite of her apparent bad behaviour, she really was a very nice girl, but unfortunately very shy.

The King and Queen were adamant that if Alicia behaved like that, she could not be his princess. Albert was so upset he had to fight back the tears – boys aren't supposed to cry, especially princes.

'She wouldn't eat or drink anything. Can't you see that she will turn into a skinny rake when she grows up? She will be so thin she won't even be able to have any children and then there will be no heirs to the throne!' bemoaned Queen Eleanor.

'No!' protested Albert. 'Alicia isn't like that, she was just shy because you are the King and Queen!'

The King shook his head. 'You must not see her again,' he said firmly.

Albert, with his head bowed down, walked slowly towards the 'Y' garden. He had suspected that Alicia wouldn't come as she had been so nervous and anxious, but was surprised to see that she was there, waiting for him.

He gave her a big hug and told her sadly that he wasn't allowed to see her any more. He would like her to come to one of his kitchens one last time – but they had to be careful.

They held hands and walked sadly towards the 'Y' kitchen, hiding amongst the yams along the way so as not to be seen.

They had a last lunch of yellow squash soup followed by a yam salad, washed down with fruity yogurt smoothies.

Yuri, the 'Y' chef, served up a yellow lemon cake and Alicia was soon back in her house, after what she presumed would be her last visit to the palace.

Chapter 26

Both Alicia and Albert were very sad and lonely.

The next morning Albert, not knowing quite what to do, went out to the 'Z' garden. As he mooched about aimlessly, he wasn't really looking where he was going and in the process he tripped over a zucchini lying on the ground.

Albert fell to the ground and cut his knee, and the sharp pain made him cry out. As his tears fell on the ground, the Fairy Godmother appeared to see if she could help him.

'You look very sad, young Albert,' she said.

'I am,' he replied. 'I don't know what to do. I have met every princess in the continent, and I don't like any of them!'

'Cheer up,' said the Fairy Godmother. 'Maybe I can help. You can have one wish which will come true. Don't forget – you must be careful what you wish for!'

'Well, I wish I was an ordinary boy living next door to Alicia,' he said, without hesitation.

And just as he made the wish, he found himself picking up a zucchini from an ordinary vegetable patch in an ordinary garden outside an ordinary little house. His mum and dad were pottering about in the garden wearing ordinary clothes and wellington boots.

His parents were not the King and Queen, and he was no longer the Prince. The wish had come true. He was just Albert, living with his mum and dad.

There was a fence at the side of the garden. Albert ran over to it and climbed up it in order to peep over the other side.

As he had hoped, there was his friend, picking a zucchini in her garden on the other side of the fence. Her mother was in the kitchen making zucchini bread. The aroma was delicious.

'Hi there!' he called over to her.

She looked up in surprise. 'Hi!' she replied. 'I'm Alicia, have you just moved in?'

'Yes!' replied Albert.

'Would you like to come round for some fruit juice?' she invited.

'I'd love to,' said Albert, and rushed round to her house as fast as he could.

They looked at each other as if they knew each other even though it seemed they were meeting for the first time… but they weren't quite sure.

They hit it off instantly and became the best of friends… forever.

Five-a-Day Fun Recipes

All recipes
serve 4 unless
otherwise
stated

Apple Crumble

What do we need?

For the filling:
- Cooking apples   450g
- Brown sugar   50g
- Cinnamon   ½ teaspoon
- Nutmeg, freshly grated
       ½ teaspoon

For the crumble topping:
- Plain flour   200g
- Butter   100g
- Sugar (caster or brown)   90g

How do we make it?

1. Preheat oven to 190°C/ Gas 5.
2. Peel and core the apples, then slice them and place them in an oven-proof bowl. Sprinkle with the brown sugar, cinnamon and nutmeg.
3. To make the crumble topping, sieve the flour into a large bowl.
4. Cut the butter into small cubes, add it to the flour and rub it between your fingers until the mixture resembles fine breadcrumbs.
5. Stir the sugar into the crumble mix, then pour it on top of the apples. Flatten gently.
6. Cook for 40 minutes in the oven or until golden brown. Delicious served with custard.

Spaghetti Bolognese

What do we need?

- Onions   2
- Celery   2 sticks
- Carrots   2
- Bacon   2 rashers
- Garlic cloves (crushed)   2
- Minced beef   500g
- Mushrooms   125g
- Tinned tomatoes   400g x 2
- Beef stock cube   1
- Bay leaves   2
- Oregano (dried)   1 teaspoon
- Worcestershire sauce   1 teaspoon
- Spaghetti   400g
- Parmesan cheese to serve (optional)

This is a good way of sneaking a few vegetables into a dish! For a vegetarian version leave out the bacon, use vegetarian mince instead of beef, and swap the beef stock cube for a veggie one.

How do we make it?

1. Finely chop the onions, celery, carrots and bacon, then fry them together until the vegetables begin to soften and the bacon is browning.
2. Add the garlic, minced beef and mushrooms and continue to fry until the mince is brown.
3. Add the tinned tomatoes, stock cube, bay leaves, oregano and Worcestershire sauce and allow to simmer for about 40 minutes.
4. Cook the spaghetti according to packet instructions. Drain and serve the spaghetti topped with the Bolognese sauce and parmesan cheese, if you like.

Carrot Cake

What do we need?

For the cake:
- Light brown sugar   175g
- Sunflower oil   175ml
- Eggs   3
- Carrots   2 large or 3 medium, grated
- Self-raising flour   175g
- Cinnamon   1 teaspoon
- Nutmeg, freshly grated   ½ teaspoon

For the icing:
- Cream cheese   150g
- Light brown sugar   50g

How do we make it?

1. Preheat the oven to 180°C/Gas 4.
2. Place the sugar in a large bowl, then pour in the oil and the eggs. Beat lightly until combined, then add the grated carrots.
3. Sift the flour, cinnamon and nutmeg into a separate bowl. Pour the eggy carrot mixture into this and mix together; you will have a fairly runny batter.
4. Pour the mixture into a lined and greased 18cm square cake tin and bake for 40-45 minutes.
5. To make the icing, beat together the cream cheese and sugar and spread on top of the cooled cake.
6. To decorate the cake as Alicia and Albert did, pipe on a 'C' in your chosen colour of icing.

Houmous

What do we need?

- Chickpeas   1 x 400g tin
- Tahini   1 tablespoon
- Garlic cloves   2, crushed
- Lemon juice   1 teaspoon

How do we make it?

1. Drain the chickpeas but keep the liquid to one side.
2. Place the chickpeas, tahini, garlic and lemon juice in a food processor or blender and whizz until blended. Add a little of the liquid from the tin of chickpeas if the houmous is too thick.

Guacamole (avocado dip)

What do we need?

- Avocados, ripe   2 large
- Lime, juice of   1
- Red onion   ½ or 1 small
- Chilli, green   1 small

How do we make it?

1. Place the avocado flesh and lime juice in a bowl and mash with a fork or a potato masher.
2. Add the onion and chilli and stir through.
3. Serve your dips with sticks of carrot, cucumber and red pepper, or strips of warmed pitta bread.

Dips

What do we need?

(Amounts given are to make one omelette that will serve 2 people)

- Eggs   4
- Butter   small knob
- Pepper   pinch
- Salt   pinch
- Cheddar cheese, grated 50g
- Tomato   1 large (eg. beef) or
      2 medium, chopped small

Cheese and Tomato Omelette

How do we make it?

1. Break the eggs into a bowl, add salt and pepper and lightly whisk them.
2. Melt a small knob of butter in a frying/omelette pan over a medium heat.
3. Pour the eggs into the pan and gently drag the mixture from the edge of the pan to the middle, until it starts to set. Then leave the egg covering the pan and let it cook for a minute or so, until the top is no longer runny but still soft.
4. Sprinkle the grated cheese and chopped tomato over one half of the omelette, then, using a spatula, fold the other half over on top of your filling. Serve immediately.

Fish Pie

What do we need?

- Skinless salmon   400g
- Haddock fillet   400g
- Milk   600ml
- Butter   100g
- Flour   50g
- Potatoes   800g
- Salt   pinch
- Pepper   pinch
- Nutmeg   ½ teaspoon
- Cheddar cheese, grated 100g
- Parsley (chopped)   25g

How do we make it?

1. Using 500ml of the milk, poach the fish in a large saucepan for 8-10 minutes.
2. Remove the fish and flake it into large pieces in a baking dish. Keep the milk to use in the sauce.
3. Boil the potatoes for 20 minutes. Drain then mash them with 50g butter and 100ml milk.
4. Melt 50g of the butter in a pan and stir in the flour. Cook for a minute. Gradually pour in the poaching milk, stirring all the time until the sauce is thick and smooth. Simmer for 5 minutes.
5. Season the sauce with salt, pepper, nutmeg and parsley and pour over the fish.
6. Top with the mashed potato, then sprinkle on the grated cheese. Bake in the oven at 200°C/Gas 6 for 30 minutes.

73

What do we need?

- Baguette   1
- Butter   100g, at room temperature
- Garlic   3 cloves
- Flat-leaf parsley   2 tablespoons, finely chopped

Garlic Bread

How do we make it?

1. Using a sharp bread knife, make diagonal cuts almost through the baguette, about 3-4cm apart.
2. Soften the butter with a wooden spoon in a bowl. Crush the garlic cloves and add to the butter along with the chopped parsley and mix well.
3. Spread the garlic butter into the slits in the baguette. Wrap loosely with foil and bake at 200°C/ Gas 6 for about 15-20 minutes.

Honey Oat Muffins

How do we make it?

1. Mix together the milk, vegetable oil, egg and honey.
2. In a large bowl, combine the dry ingredients.
3. Stir the milk and oil mixture into the dry ingredients, mixing until just combined. Don't overmix.
4. Fill muffin cases ⅔ full and bake at 200°C/Gas 6 for 15-18 minutes.

What do we need?

- Milk   160ml
- Vegetable oil   80ml
- Egg   1, beaten
- Honey   60ml
- Rolled oats   125g
- Wholemeal flour   125g
- Raisins   100g
- Baking powder   1 teaspoon
- Cinnamon   1 teaspoon

What do we need?

- Raspberries (also works well with blackberries, strawberries or blackcurrants)   450g
- Condensed milk   100ml
- Double cream   142ml pot

Ice Cream

How do we make it?

1. Place 375g of the raspberries in a blender and whizz to a puree.
2. Add the condensed milk and double cream and blend again.
3. Add the remaining raspberries and just pulse once or twice, so you get some pieces of fruit in the finished ice cream.
4. Pour the mixture into a freezable container and freeze overnight. Remove from the freezer about half an hour before serving.

Juicy Fruit Drinks

What do we need?

- Oranges   2
- Mangoes   2
- Ice cubes   handful

Any choice of fruits will make delicious fruit juice drinks. Orange and mango, as given here, is a great combination, so is strawberry and banana.

How do we make it?

1. Peel the oranges and remove the central stone and skin from the mangoes. Cut the peeled fruits into smallish pieces and place in a blender.
2. Add a glass full of ice cubes to the blender.
3. Run the blender for 5 minutes.
4. Pour the drinks into glasses and enjoy!

Kiwi Tart

How do we make it?

1. Preheat the oven to 200°C/ Gas 6.
2. Line a baking tin with the pastry. This amount would fit a 23cm diameter round tin, or you could use two smaller heart-shaped tins, like Alicia does.
3. Cover the pastry base with greaseproof paper and baking beans (or pieces of scrunched up kitchen foil) and bake 'blind' for 10 minutes. Allow to cool before adding the filling.
4. Mix the mascarpone cheese with the sugar, milk, lime zest and vanilla extract and spread over the cooled pastry base.
5. Decorate with slices of kiwi fruit in whatever pattern you choose and leave in the fridge for at least an hour before serving.

What do we need?

- Sweet shortcrust pastry
    1 x 320g sheet, ready rolled
- Mascarpone cheese   150g
- Caster sugar   2 tablespoons
- Milk   2 tablespoons
- Lime zest   1 teaspoon
- Vanilla extract   a few drops
- Kiwis   4

What do we need?

- Linguine 300g
- Olive oil 2 tablespoons
- Garlic clove 1, crushed
- Stock (fish or vegetable) 100ml
- White crabmeat 1 x 170g tin
- Prawns 300g, cooked and peeled
- Lemon, juice of 1
- Parsley 2 tablespoons, finely chopped

How do we make it?

1. Cook the linguine according to the packet instructions.
2. In a large saucepan, heat the oil and gently fry the garlic in it. Add the stock and simmer for a couple of minutes.
3. Add the remaining ingredients to the pan, including the cooked, drained pasta and mix well before serving.

Lemon and Seafood Linguine

Meringues with Fresh Fruit

What do we need?

- Egg whites   3
- Caster sugar   175g
- Double cream   150ml
- Mixed fresh fruit, chopped, eg. mangoes, mandarins, melons, strawberries

How do we make it?

1. Preheat oven to 130°C/ Gas 1.
2. In a perfectly clean, grease-free bowl, whisk the egg whites until they form stiff peaks.
3. Gradually whisk in the sugar, adding about a tablespoon at a time. Keep whisking until the mixture is glossy and still stiff.
4. Line a baking tray with greaseproof paper or baking parchment. Put dessertspoon-size dollops on the tray and place them in the oven. Bake for about 1 hour and leave them in the oven to dry out as it cools.
5. When the meringues are cold, serve them with chopped fruit and whipped cream.

Nut Loaf

What do we need?

- Brown rice   100g
- Vegetable oil   2 tablespoons
- Onion   1, chopped
- Garlic clove   2, crushed
- Carrots   2 large, diced
- Chestnut mushrooms
    175g, chopped
- Plain flour   2 tablespoons
- Cashew nuts   50g
- Walnuts   50g
- Almonds   50g
- Brazil nuts   50g
- Breadcrumbs   115g
- Egg   1
- Cheddar cheese 115g, grated
- Oregano   1 teaspoon
- Basil   1 teaspoon
- Salt and pepper

How do we make it?

1. Preheat oven to 180°C/ Gas 4.
2. Boil the brown rice according to the packet instructions.
3. Fry the chopped onions, carrots, mushrooms and garlic in the vegetable oil for 5 minutes, until becoming soft.
4. Stir in 1 tablespoon of flour to this vegetable mixture, the all the chopped nuts.
5. Mix in the breadcrumbs, beaten egg, herbs, salt and pepper and cheese and remove from the heat.
6. Bring the mixture together into a loaf shape, sprinkle with flour and place on a greased baking tray.
7. Bake for 50-60 minutes.

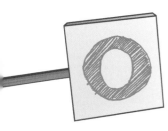

Orange and Carrot Soup

What do we need?

- Sunflower oil   1 tablespoon
- Onion   1, chopped
- Carrots   600g, chopped
- Vegetable stock   1 litre
- Oranges   2, juice and zest of
- Salt and pepper

How do we make it?

1. Heat the oil in a large saucepan. Add the onion and carrots and cook for about 5 minutes, until becoming soft.
2. Add the orange zest and cook for another couple of minutes.
3. Add the stock, salt and pepper and bring to the boil. Simmer until the vegetables are tender – about 10-15 minutes.
4. Liquidise the soup in a blender, then stir in the orange juice. Reheat to serve.

How do we make it?

1. Line a 23cm diameter flan case with the pastry.
2. Cut the pumpkin into quarters and remove the seeds. Lightly brush the insides with vegetable oil, place on an oiled baking tray and roast at 160°C/ Gas 3 for about 30 minutes. Allow to cool slightly then mash the flesh with the butter.
3. In a large bowl beat the eggs, then add the brown sugar, spices, mashed pumpkin and double cream.
4. Bake at 180°C/Gas 4 for 35-40 minutes.
5. Chill in the fridge overnight and serve with whipped cream or crème fraiche.

What do we need?

- Pumpkin 1 large – you want about 450g flesh
- Vegetable oil   1 tablespoon
- Sweet shortcrust pastry
  1 x 320g sheet, ready rolled
- Butter   75g
- Eggs   2
- Brown sugar   75g
- Cinnamon   1 teaspoon
- Nutmeg, freshly grated
  ½ teaspoon
- Ginger, ground ½ teaspoon
- Cloves, ground ¼ teaspoon
- Double cream   150ml

Pumpkin Pie

 # Summer Quiche

What do we need?

- Shortcrust pastry
  1 x 320g sheet, ready rolled
- Vegetable oil   25g
- Butter   25g
- Courgettes, sliced   90g
- Runner beans, sliced   90g
- Peas, fresh or frozen   90g
- Spring onions, sliced   3
- Plain flour   25g
- Double cream   150ml
- Milk   150ml
- Mint
  1 tablespoon, finely chopped
- Eggs   2
- Salt and pepper
- Feta cheese   100g

How do we make it?

1. Line a 23cm flan case with the pastry.
2. Melt the oil and butter in a saucepan and cook the spring onions, runner beans, peas and courgettes in it for about 5 minutes.
3. Stir in the flour and cook for one minute, then pour in the milk and cream. Keep stirring while this cooks until it thickens. Add the mint, then remove from the heat.
4. Beat the eggs and season with salt and pepper. Stir these into the vegetable mix and then pour it into the pastry case.
5. Scatter crumbled feta cheese over the filling then cook the quiche in the oven at 190°C/Gas 5 for 35-40 minutes.

Raspberry fool

What do we need?

- Raspberries   300g
- Icing sugar, sieved   50g
- Double cream   280ml

How do we make it?

1. Whisk the double cream until it forms soft peaks.
2. Put a few raspberries aside to place whole on top of your finished fool. Mash the remaining raspberries with a fork then stir in the icing sugar.
3. Fold the raspberry mixture into the whipped cream, then spoon into serving glasses. Place one or two whole raspberries on top of each.

What do we need?

- Strawberries   225g
- Strawberry jelly
                  1 pack/sachet
- Swiss roll   1, ideally
    filled with strawberry jam
  and buttercream (bought) or
    half a home-made Victoria
              sandwich cake
- Caster sugar   2 tablespoons
- Custard powder
              2 tablespoons
- Milk   570ml
- Double cream   300 ml

Strawberry Trifle

How do we make it?

1. Make the jelly according to the packet instructions.
2. Slice the Swiss roll or sponge cake and place at the bottom of a trifle dish. Scatter the strawberries on top, then pour the jelly over. Leave to set.
3. In a measuring jug, mix the caster sugar and custard powder with 2-3 tablespoons of milk taken from the 570ml.
4. Heat the remaining milk in a saucepan until nearly boiling, then pour it onto the custard powder mixture. Tip it back into the saucepan and, on a gentle heat, keep stirring while it thickens.
5. Leave the custard to cool slightly (but keep stirring so a skin doesn't form) then pour it on top of the trifle. Leave to set.
6. Whip the cream until soft peaks are formed and dollop on top of the custard. Decorate with strawberry slices.

Tomato and Tuna Pizza

What do we need?

For the base:
- Plain flour   375g
- Salt   ½ teaspoon
- Easy blend yeast
                          1 x 7g sachet
- Olive oil   30 ml
- Warm water   225ml
- Topping:
- Tomato puree   100g
- Tomatoes   4, chopped
- Tuna   185 g
- Cheese (chopped or sliced mozzarella is great on pizza, or you could use grated Cheddar)   200g

The great thing about pizza is that you can customise it to suit yourself, so play around with different toppings.

How do we make it?

1. Mix the flour, salt and yeast in a large bowl, then slowly add the warm water and olive oil.
2. Knead the mixture with your hands on a floured worktop for about 5 minutes, until it is smooth and stretchy.
3. Place the dough in a clean bowl, cover it with a tea towel and leave it somewhere warm to rise for 1 hour.
4. After an hour, knead the dough again, then leave to rise for a further 30 minutes. Then it's ready to roll out and top; this amount will make one large or two smaller pizza bases.
5. Spread tomato puree over the pizza base, then add the chopped tomatoes followed by flaked tuna and a pinch of pepper. Sprinkle the cheese on top.
6. Bake in the oven at 200°C/ Gas 6 for 15-20 minutes depending on how crispy you like it!

Upside-Down Cake

What do we need?

- Butter or margarine 100g, plus extra for greasing the tin
- Brown sugar 25g
- Pineapple slices 1 x 432g tin
- Glace cherries 75g
- Caster sugar 100g
- Eggs 2
- Vanilla extract a few drops
- Self-raising flour 100g
- Baking powder 1 teaspoon

How do we make it?

1. Grease a large, round cake tin, then sprinkle the brown sugar in the base.
2. Place the pineapple slices on the base of the tin, and pop a glace cherry in the centre of each.
3. Cream the butter and caster sugar until light and fluffy.
4. Beat the eggs then add them to the sugar mix, along with the vanilla extract.
5. Gradually fold in the sieved flour, then place this sponge mix on top of the pineapple slices.
6. Bake in the oven at 180°C/ Gas 4 for 30-35 minutes.

What do we need?

- Potatoes   300g
- Onion   1 large
- Carrots   100g
- Celery   50g
- Sweet potatoes   100g
- Vegetable stock   750ml
- Olive oil   2 tablespoons
- Parsley   1 tablespoon
- Salt and pepper

How do we make it?

1. Chop the potatoes, carrots, onion, celery and sweet potatoes into small chunks of roughly the same size.
2. Heat the oil in a large pan and add all the vegetables. Cook for 5-10 minutes until they begin to soften.
3. Add the vegetable stock and simmer the mixture for about 15 minutes, until all the vegetables are tender. Add the parsley and seasoning.
4. Liquidise the soup and reheat to serve.

Vegetable Soup

What do we need?

- Flour tortillas 4
- Cooked chicken 250g
- Streaky bacon
   .... 4 rashers, grilled
- Avocado ...... 1 (2 if small)
- Spinach, shredded
   .... 2 handfuls
- Mayonnaise or tomato salsa
   1 dessertspoon per tortilla

How do we make it?

1. Place some shredded spinach on top of each tortilla.
2. Chop the cooked chicken and bacon quite small and divide between the four tortillas.
3. Spoon tomato salsa or mayonnaise (or both if you like!) on top of the meat, then top with slices of avocado.
4. Wrap up each tortilla fairly tightly so that the filling stays in.

Chicken, Bacon and Avocado Wraps

Xigua Melon Medley

What do we need?

- Xigua melon   1
- Oranges   2
- Grapes, seedless   100g
- Tangerines   4, segmented
- Strawberries   200g
- Pineapple chunks
      1 x 432g tin, in own juice
- Raspberries   200g
- Bananas   2, sliced
- Apples   2, sliced

How do we make it?

1. Cut the Xigua melon in the shape of a basket, creating an integral decorative handle out of the outer skin on the top half.
2. Partially scoop out the centre of the basket and chop up some of the flesh.
3. Squeeze out the juice from the oranges into the basket
4. Then simply fill the melon basket with your colourful array of berries and chopped fruit.

Yogurt smoothies

These are incredibly simple to make with your favourite fruits and yogurt. Just peel and chop your fruit and whizz it up in a food processor with the yogurt and sometimes some milk or fruit juice. Here are some suggestions for yummy combinations:

1

- 1 banana
- 1 small pot fruits of the forest yogurt
- 1 handful of frozen fruits of the forest

2

- 1 large mango
- half a banana
- 250ml natural yogurt
- 150ml milk

3

- 1 banana
- 2 apples (peeled, cored and chopped)
- 1 pear (peeled, cored and chopped)
- 250ml vanilla yogurt
- 250ml apple juice
- pinch of cinnamon

4

- 90g raspberries
- 100ml cranberry juice
- 50ml milk
- 100ml natural yogurt
- 1 tablespoon caster sugar

Zucchini (Courgette) Bread

Makes one loaf

What do we need?

- Butter   200g
- Brown sugar   200g
- Eggs   3
- Zucchini (courgettes)
                        200g, grated
- Walnuts 50g, finely chopped
- Plain flour   200g
- Baking powder   1 teaspoon
- Cinnamon   1 teaspoon

How do we make it?

1. Preheat oven to 170°C/ Gas 3.
2. Melt the butter in a small saucepan.
3. In a large bowl whisk the eggs, then gradually add in the brown sugar, continuing to whisk until combined well and smooth.
4. Add the grated courgettes to the egg and sugar mix.
5. In another bowl, sift the flour with the baking powder and cinnamon.
6. Add the courgette mix and the walnuts to the bowl of flour and mix until just combined.
7. Pour the mix into a greased and lined loaf tin and bake in the oven for 45-50 minutes.

Health notes by Max Denning

Background

A great deal of research has been conducted into the importance of good nutrition, especially its effects on young children. Although research is continually evolving, the essential aspects of nutrition have been long appreciated. Children need to eat a healthy balanced diet in addition to leading an active lifestyle. This means getting the right balance of macronutrients such as carbohydrates, protein and fats. Vitamins and minerals are also essential in small quantities.

This book aims to provide advice and guidance in a fun way. Extra notes are provided in this section for parents, while simple recipes are included that children can participate in preparing. It is hoped this will help to introduce them to a wide variety of foods whilst encouraging fruit and vegetable intake and a generally healthy, balanced diet.

Obesity trends have been rising rapidly in the Western world and this poses a number of health risks. It is important that parents, teachers and carers educate children about a healthy diet - forming habits that will last into adulthood. The government has a number of initiatives in place to combat obesity through improving diet and physical activity, such as tight regulations on the advertising of junk foods, advertising campaigns advocating healthy eating, discounted exercise initiatives and access to free advice; however, these alone are not sufficient. Notably, whilst the media proclaim the dangers of

obesity, it is important that health, and not 'skinnyness' is sought after. Popular magazines put pressure on children and adults alike to be thin, but a compromise should be sought. Being underweight is equally dangerous. The cautionary tale of eating little or nothing is depicted by the King and Queen's vision of what Alicia would be like if she didn't eat. She would be too thin to have a healthy life and would suffer from a whole range of vitamin and mineral deficiencies. Everyone has an ideal weight that is dictated by his or her genetics, height and physical activity level amongst other factors.

It is important, especially in growing children, to have a balanced diet that delivers everything required for healthy growth. Calorie-restricted dieting is not recommended in children. Rather a varied diet in which all the essential micro- and macronutrients are supplied and junk food high in salt, trans fats, sugar and additives are avoided. It is advisable to substitute snacks and sugary drinks for healthier alternatives, such as fruit, nuts, seeds, or low fat yoghurt.

Recent findings have shown that childhood eating habits influence eating in later life. It has even been shown that what women eat and do whilst pregnant can influence the eating patterns of their children later on in life due to 'in utero programming'! Diets high in sugar and e-numbers have been suggested to contribute to behavioural problems in children, many of which can be remedied with improved diet.

1 – Cancer prevention

One of the biggest studies into diet and cancer risk is the European Prospective Investigation into Cancer and Nutrition (EPIC), a collaboration between many European countries. It has been found that a diet low in animal fats and high in fibre can reduce the risk of cancer attributed to dietary causes by up to a half. High fibre diets have been shown to decrease the risk of colon and stomach cancer. Likewise, low levels of salt show correlations with a decreased risk of gastric and other cancers as well as lower rates of heart disease. The key to a longer and healthier life is for parents to get their children to start eating wisely as early as possible.

2 – Achieving a balance

The recipes in this book have been selected for their nutritional value, ease of preparation with the help of children and to encourage them to try different, tasty and healthy foods.

Children love rolling out pastry or pizza bases, mixing ingredients and using kitchen utensils under adult supervision. This book is designed for children to see how the food they enjoy cooking can be part of a healthy balanced diet, educating at the same time as being fun. One way of making the most of the book is to read one chapter at a time on the same day as preparing the corresponding recipe suggestion.

Sugar has been included in small amounts in some recipes, but for a healthy alternative this can be substituted for honey, agave nectar, or natural sweeteners such as stevia. Likewise cream is in a small number of the recipes, but this can be substituted for low-fat alternatives such as reduced fat coconut milk (if forming the base of a sauce), full cream milk or reduced fat versions of cream. While excessive usage of sugar and cream is not encouraged, small quantities incorporated into a balanced diet will not be deleterious and may help to make certain foods more palatable to young children.

Children tend to self-regulate the amount of food they eat, therefore it is important to combine their daily intake into smaller 'me-size' portions, providing healthy balanced meals three times a day – and substituting unhealthy snacking with fruit and vegetables – the 'naturally fast foods'.

Take special caution with regard to fizzy drinks, especially cola drinks, which are loaded with sugar and can dissolve away teeth or cause weight gain as depicted by Princess Pearl in chapter sixteen. Soft drinks and indeed drinks in general are often overlooked when considering a diet, but a single can of cola can contain up to 40% of the recommended daily allowance (RDA) of sugar for an adult, which equates to over 50% of the RDA a child should have in a day. Try to encourage water, no added sugar fruit squashes or natural fruit juices and smoothies, which are packed full of vitamins and minerals whilst being naturally sweet.

3 – A varied diet

Dietary deficiencies are rare in the Western world; it takes very small quantities of vitamins and minerals to sustain a healthy diet. Vitamin supplements are not recommended in children, and so a balanced, varied intake of fruit and vegetables should ensure that they get what they need.

Omega 3 fatty acids and other essential fatty acids (EFAs) are required for good nerve and brain development in infants and young children. These can be obtained by eating oily fish such as salmon, mackerel, fresh tuna and herring. Recent studies have also alluded to a role for EFAs in improving cognitive function in adolescents and geriatrics after the majority of brain development has been completed.

Fruit, vegetables and fibre have been shown to lower the rate of stomach and bowel cancer, whereas an excess of red meat (more then twice a week) has been shown to increase the rate of bowel cancer.

4 – Vitamin deficiencies

Dietary deficiencies were first described by Hippocrates some 2,500 years ago. He described a 'herbal cure' for scurvy, a disease which we now know is caused by **vitamin C** deficiency. Sailors in the British Navy used to eat limes at sea to help prevent scurvy, hence the nickname 'limies'.

It was not until 1936 that vitamin C was finally isolated and identified as an essential component of a healthy diet and found to be a key ingredient in citrus fruits. Since then, other vitamins and minerals have been isolated.

Vitamin A deficiency can affect vision. Carrots are particularly helpful to protect against this, as they are rich in vitamin A, as are a number of other foods such as sweet potato, liver, pumpkin seeds, eggs, broccoli and spinach. 'Carrots make you see in the dark' was a saying that originated in World War Two, due to the abundance of carrots that were available at the time. Retinol is the active form

of vitamin A and is a pigment that is required for both night and colour vision. However only small amounts of vitamin A are needed for normal vision and a healthy intake of carrots, squash, green vegetables and dairy products should meet all normal vision requirements.

The problems of a vitamin A deficiency are depicted in chapter three, where Princess Catherine can't see the steps up to the coronation chair and trips up as a result!

There are various types of **Vitamin B** deficiency, each causing varying symptoms:

· B1 deficiency causes lethargy and heart problems.

· B2 deficiency gives rise to vision problems.

· B3 deficiency can lead to skin and mouth problems.

· B6 deficiency results in itchy, scaly, patchy skin with eventual hair loss, as suffered by Princess Karen.

· B12 deficiency leads to pernicious anaemia, which is rare.

Vitamin D is synthesised in the body from sunlight falling on the skin. It can also be acquired through the consumption of fortified dairy, mushrooms, oily fish or eggs. Vitamin D deficiency was very common some sixty years ago and was the reason why free milk was introduced to all school children.

Rickets is a result of vitamin D deficiency in children, which weakens bones and causes bow legs, as depicted by Princess Madeleine in chapter fourteen. There has been a recent increase in the incidence of rickets due to decreasing trends of milk consumption and sun exposure. It is, however, important to protect children from too much sun by applying sun lotion of factor thirty to fifty (but not completely rubbing it into the skin) especially between the hours of 11 a.m. – 3 p.m. when the sun is strongest. It is best for children to get some sunlight in the early morning or late evening in summer and whenever possible in winter.

Vitamin K is important for blood coagulation and is often given to newborn babies to prevent bleeding disorders. It is found in green leafy vegetables, nuts and seeds.

5 – Salt in the diet

Excess salt has been linked to heart and blood pressure problems. Epidemiological studies have also found a correlation to high rates (two- to three-fold increase) of stomach cancer in the Japanese. Ready meals frequently contain high levels of salt to improve flavour. White bread, crisps and preserved meats such as biltong or ham are also high in salt. Beware the amount of extra salt ingested by children from foods like salted crisps and chips!

A small amount of salt is necessary for the body to function normally, although adequate amounts are usually found naturally occurring in foods. Salt is important to replace the electrolytes lost in sweat during exercise. Loss of excessive salt can cause cramps. If cramps are experienced during exercise, then consider taking an isotonic sports drink to prevent dehydration and replenish lost electrolytes. These are available from most food stores.

6 – Obesity

Obesity, defined as having a body mass index greater than thirty, increases the risk of major diseases including heart disease, strokes, diabetes, arthritis and certain cancers. A contributing factor to the current 'obesity epidemic' is increasing trends of 'junk food' consumption, offering little nutritional value with high calorific loads. Weight gain can be avoided by ensuring an active lifestyle in conjunction with healthy meals as outlined in this book.

Many parents frequently ask if it is bad to let children have a treat occasionally. While this will not cause obesity as a one-off event, there is a danger of creating habits and shifting the palate of children to sweeter, less healthy foods. Once all of the necessary micro- and macronutrients for a day have been consumed, if there is a calorie deficit, this can be made up with what is called 'discretionary calories'. This allows for treats with little nutritional value to be consumed and in fact this is encouraged in the healthy diet of young children. USDA suggests that young children can consume between 160-190 'discretionary' kCal per day, allowing for one or two snacks. These do not need to be in the form of chocolate bars or crisps though! Far better are healthy flapjacks, granola with yoghurt, or oatmeal and raisin cookies, for example. The American heart foundation, however, recommends that the calories from sugar consumed per day should not exceed half of the discretionary calories. 4kCal are present in every 1g of sugar, suggesting that the total sugar consumption for an entire day should not exceed 40-45g sugar. Young children require a total of around 1000kCal per day, but this varies with genetics, sex, height and activity level.

7 – Extra help

Some parents find they have problems getting hold of good-quality information on diet. For those with Internet access, the government runs a number of websites that have been edited by nutrition experts. These provide information in a very accessible format – a list of suggestions is shown below. However, if in doubt, simply search on the Internet and a barrage of helpful websites will appear. There are also many useful books that can give more in depth information.

Useful websites:

• http://www.nhs.uk/Change4Life/Pages/change-for-life.aspx

• http://www.nhs.uk/livewell/healthy-eating/Pages/Healthyeating.aspx

• http://www.direct.gov.uk/en/YoungPeople/HealthAndRelationships/KeepingHealthy/DG_10030623

• livestrong.com

• schoolfoodtrust.org.uk

• Some interesting dessert recipes can be found at http://chockohlawtay.blogspot.co.uk/

One frequently-asked question is whether dietary supplements are necessary. While those such as multivitamins and cod liver oil are useful in certain situations and some have general benefits after illness, they are not replacements for a healthy balanced diet. Most authorities argue that all the essentials can be acquired from a balanced diet without supplements.

Five-a-day is a long-running government initiative to ensure that adequate levels of essential vitamins, minerals and roughage are consumed. This can be crudely achieved through the consumption of 5 portions of different 'fruit and veg' every day: that is not to say that it is bad to aim for more than 5! The government's more recent Change4Life scheme encourages healthy eating and higher levels of physical activity to counteract a TV/computer-orientated and generally more sedentary lifestyle that has been observed across all age groups.

8 – Organic produce

Wherever possible, it is preferable to use organic produce since not all common pesticides have been studied fully enough to reveal any long-term health effects. However, organic food is not always available and is more costly therefore if you are using non-organic food, it is important that the outside is washed well to remove any invisible chemical residues.